To my sisters, Jean, Polly, and Lisa   KH
For Katharine, with love and thanks for years of fun with Angelina   HC

Published by Pleasant Company Publications
© 2000 HIT Entertainment PLC
Text copyright © 1991 Katharine Holabird
Illustrations copyright © 1991 Helen Craig

All rights reserved. No part of this book may be used or reproduced in any
manner whatsoever without written permission except in the case of
brief quotations embodied in critical articles and reviews.
For information, address: Book Editor, Pleasant Company Publications,
8400 Fairway Place, P.O. Box 620998, Middleton, Wisconsin 53562.

Visit our Web site at **americangirl.com** and Angelina's very own site at **angelinaballerina.com**

Second Edition
Printed in Italy.
01 02 03 04 05 06 LEGO 10 9 8 7 6 5 4

Library of Congress Cataloging-in-Publication Data
Craig, Helen.
Angelina's baby sister / illustrations by Helen Craig ;
story by Katharine Holabird.
p. cm.
Summary: Angelina's excitement over the arrival of a
new baby turns to jealousy when her little sister
becomes the center of attention.
ISBN 1-58485-132-5
[1. Babies—Fiction. 2. Sisters—Fiction. 3. Mice—Fiction.]
I. Holabird, Katharine. II. Title.
PZ7.C84418 Apf 2000
[E]—dc21   00-022881

Angelina's Baby Sister

Story by **Katharine Holabird** Illustrations by **Helen Craig**

PLEASANT COMPANY PUBLICATIONS™

Angelina was so excited. Very soon there was going to be a new baby in the family! Angelina couldn't wait to be a big sister, and it was hard to think about anything else—even when Miss Lilly gave Angelina a beautiful china statue as a prize at ballet school.

"Perhaps you can make up a dance to welcome the baby," suggested Miss Lilly when Angelina thanked her. Angelina raced home to show her mother the lovely prize.

Angelina ran so fast that she almost bumped into Dr. Tuttle as he was leaving. "Your mother is resting upstairs," he said, "and she has a surprise for you…"

Angelina leapt up the stairs and into the bedroom—and there were her parents, gazing lovingly at the newborn baby.

"Her name is Polly," said Mrs. Mouseling happily. "Would you like to hold her?" Angelina couldn't believe how delicate her little sister was.

"I'll be a good big sister, Polly," Angelina said softly, as she rocked the baby in her arms.

Angelina's father smiled at her. "We know you will," he said.

That evening Angelina and her father made supper while Mrs. Mouseling stayed in bed with Polly.

"Don't worry. Pretty soon your mother will be up and around again," said Angelina's father, "but now we have to take good care of her."

Angelina felt sad and confused. Why should one little baby need so much attention and make her mother feel so tired?

Angelina played with the pretty china dancer. Before she went to sleep she placed it carefully on her dresser where she could show it to her mother.

But the next day Angelina's mother was so busy looking after the new baby that there was no time to look at Angelina's prize, and the day after that Polly sneezed several times and Dr. Tuttle came back to see that she didn't catch a cold.

Mr. Mouseling was a good cook, but Angelina
missed her mother's special Cheddar cheese
pies after school. Having a baby sister
was not at all the way Angelina
had imagined it would be!

A whole week went by. Angelina
went to school every day and
tried to be good while
everyone fussed over
Polly, but it was
very hard.

The weekend came, and Angelina's grandparents arrived to visit. Angelina could hardly wait to see them again. When the doorbell rang she raced to answer it. "Grandma! Grandpa!" she shouted, "just look at this!"

Angelina started to show her grandparents her new dance, but Grandma hugged Angelina quickly and said, "Wait just a minute, Angelina dear, first we have to see the baby!"

They went upstairs and Angelina could hear everyone laughing and talking together. She stamped her foot as loudly as she could, but nobody heard her. She tried to do a few steps of her dance but it seemed stupid and clumsy. Upstairs Grandpa was tickling Polly's toes.

"Isn't she just adorable!" Grandma exclaimed.

"Angelina—come and join us!" called her father. But Angelina didn't want to go and see Polly. At that moment she hated Polly and wished Polly would just disappear!

Angelina was so upset that she stomped to her room and slammed the door. Still nobody came. Angelina felt absolutely miserable. She was sure that nobody cared about her any more. Grandma and Grandpa didn't even want to see her dance!

Angelina grabbed one of her stuffed toys and threw it as hard as she could across the room, where it landed with a thud. Then she threw another and another. Angelina threw all of her stuffed toys and all of her dolls. Then she threw all her papers and crayons. She jumped up and down on her bed and she gave her dresser a terrific kick. The dresser shook, and down fell the china dancer, where it broke on the floor and lay in pieces.

"ANGELINA!"

Everyone was standing at the door. Angelina threw herself on her bed and burst into tears. Mrs. Mouseling sat down on the bed and took Angelina in her arms.

"You were just as sweet as Polly when you were a baby," Angelina's mother smiled, "but now that you're bigger and we can do things together I love you more than ever."

"I just wanted to do my new dance and show you my beautiful prize—but I got so angry I broke it!!" Angelina pointed at the broken china dancer and cried even harder.

"I know someone who can fix it," said Mrs. Mouseling, and she gave the little figure to Grandpa, who went off to get the glue.

"You promised to show us a dance," Grandma said, smiling, "and we've been waiting all this time."

Slowly Angelina began to feel better. "I guess it's not so easy to get used to being a big sister," she admitted, wiping her tears away. Grandma and Grandpa helped Angelina pick up her toys and they all went downstairs for tea.

Mrs. Mouseling had baked Angelina's favorite Cheddar cheese pies. "I wanted to surprise you," she said.

Then Mr. Mouseling played his fiddle and Angelina did her special dance to welcome her baby sister, while Polly giggled with delight.

That night, Angelina showed Polly her favorite book, and helped put her to bed. "You know," she whispered, "when you get bigger I'm going to teach you to dance, too!"

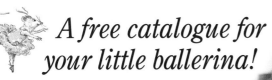

A free catalogue for your little ballerina!

If you've fallen in love with Angelina Ballerina,™ you'll love the American Girl catalogue. Angelina's world comes to life in a line of charming playthings and girl-sized clothes that complement her beautiful books. You'll also discover Bitty Baby,® a precious baby doll with her own adorable clothes and accessories.

To receive your free catalogue, return this card, visit our Web site at **americangirl.com**, or call **1-800-845-0005**.

Send me a catalogue:

Name

Address

City   State   Zip

                                                            86945i

My child's birth date: _____ / _____ / _____
                        month   day   year

Send my friend a catalogue:

Name

Address

City   State   Zip

                                                            86947i

American Girl™

PO BOX 620497
MIDDLETON WI 53562-0497

Place
Stamp
Here